92

PiPPi
Longstocking in the Park

by Astrid Lindgren
with Pictures by Ingrid Nyman

R&S
BOOKS

Stockholm New York London Adelaide Toronto

Rabén & Sjögren Bokförlag, Stockholm
http://www.raben.se

Translation copyright © 2001 by Rabén & Sjögren Bokförlag
Text copyright © 1949 by Astrid Lindgren
Illustrations copyright © 1949 by Ingrid Vang Nyman
All rights reserved
Originally published in Sweden by Rabén & Sjögren
under the title *Pippi Långstrump i Humlegården*

Library of Congress catalog card number: 00-135405
Printed in Denmark
First American edition, 2001

ISBN 91-29-65307-X

The little tiny town where Pippi Longstocking lived was a very peaceful place. There were only a few bullies. And Pippi soon taught them a lesson!

But it was terrible in the big city. The newspaper was full of stories about the bad guys there.

"Look what it says here," said Tommy, and pointed in the newspaper so that Pippi could see.

Terrible bad-guy activities in the park at night. The police are powerless.

"Bad, bad," said Pippi, and poked her head thoughtfully out of the firewood chest.

Pippi and Tommy and Annika sat in Villa Villekulla's firewood chest when they read the paper.

"They need a Pippi Longstocking in that park," said Annika.

"If you think so," said Pippi, "they'll get one. We'll move to the park."

"Are you crazy," said Tommy. "We can't do that. Where will we live? It's not as if we can go sleep at the Royal Library!"

"We'll bring Villa Villekulla along," said Pippi. "I can tear it down and build it again in an afternoon."

"But . . ." said Annika, surprised.

"We're going," said Pippi. "I get so sad when I hear that the police are powerless."

"But you'll move Villa Villekulla back afterward?" asked Tommy suspiciously. "After you've taken care of all the bad guys in the City Park?"

Pippi nodded.

That's how it happened. Pippi and Tommy and Annika and Mr. Nilsson, Pippi's little monkey, and the horse and a lot of boards – which had been Villa Villekulla – arrived one afternoon in the City Park in the center of Stockholm. Pippi went right to work and built the house precisely as it had been in the old yard in the little tiny town.

When the house was almost finished, and it was only missing the roof, an angry little man in a gray suit came walking down the path.

"Do you have permission to build that?" he asked, and pointed at Villa Villekulla.

"What?" asked Pippi.

"Permission to build," shouted the man in gray. "Permission to build! Do you have permission?"

"No," said Pippi. "But so far we've managed anyway."

The biggest of the bad guys was especially nasty; he was called the Heel. "No ride," said the Heel, and kicked the horse so that it would get off the porch. "No ride, you say. Who's going to stop me?"

He laughed nastily and was about to pull himself up onto the horse.

"Just a minute," said Pippi. "Can I ask you something before you get up on my horse?"

"What?" asked the Heel.

"Well, I was just wondering where you'd like to be buried after I'm through with you, here in the City Park or somewhere else?"

The Heel laughed even more nastily and jumped up on the horse.

When he woke up, he was lying in the grass at the other end of the park with all the other bad guys. They lay in a tidy little pile and could not move, because their legs and arms were tied with strong ropes.

"What happened?" asked the Heel in a weak voice. "Was it an earthquake?"

At first, no one answered. But at last, Casper, one of the other bad guys, said, "She . . . the red-haired kid . . . she . . . Oh, oh, oh!"

"You don't mean that she was the one who . . ." said the Heel.

"Exactly," said Casper.

The Heel gritted his teeth and tried without luck to get loose.

"Grrr," he growled. "If I was as strong as Superman, that girl would see something else."

"Pal," said Casper, "Superman wouldn't have a chance against that girl."

Pippi had disappeared. She was calling the police from a phone booth. "May I speak with the chief of police?" she asked politely.

The woman who answered the phone at the police station could tell that she was speaking with a child.

"You want to speak with Chief Ross?" she asked suspiciously.

"If you have another chief handy, I can speak with him first," said Pippi. But the woman didn't, and Chief Ross came on the line.

"Chief," said Pippi, "This is Pippi Longstocking. I have a pile of bad guys tied up in the park. Should I carry them over to the police station, or will you come get them?"

The Chief was thrilled and sent a couple of police cars over to the park right away. And he said that he would like to continue to work with Pippi.

"Just call, then we'll make a pickup," he said with satisfaction, and hung up.

Finally, there would be peace and quiet in the City Park!

Soon after that, it was Children's Day in the park. And since Pippi thought that there would probably be a lot of children from Stockholm who would like to meet her and Tommy and Annika and look at Villa Villekulla, she decided to stay in the city for a few more days. Perhaps there were also some children who would like to ride on her horse and meet Mr. Nilsson.

Mr. Nilsson had a very fine visitor on Children's Day.

His relative, the large gorilla Mr. Svensson, came from Kurrekurredut Island. Mr. Svensson was a very unusual ape, as the children of Stockholm could see for themselves.

Yes, there was always something to look at in the City Park.